This edition published in 1994 by
SMITHMARK Publishers Inc.,
16 East 32nd Street, New York,
NY 10016.

SMITHMARK books are available for bulk purchase for
sales promotion and premium use. For details write or call
the manager of special sales, SMITHMARK Publishers Inc.,
16 East 32nd Street, New York,
NY 10016; (212) 532-6600.

Produced by Brompton Books Inc.
15 Sherwood Place
Greenwich, CT 06830

ISBN 0-8317-1666-5

Printed in Hong Kong

10 9 8 7 6 5 4 3 2 1

"VAN GOOL'S"

Sleeping Beauty

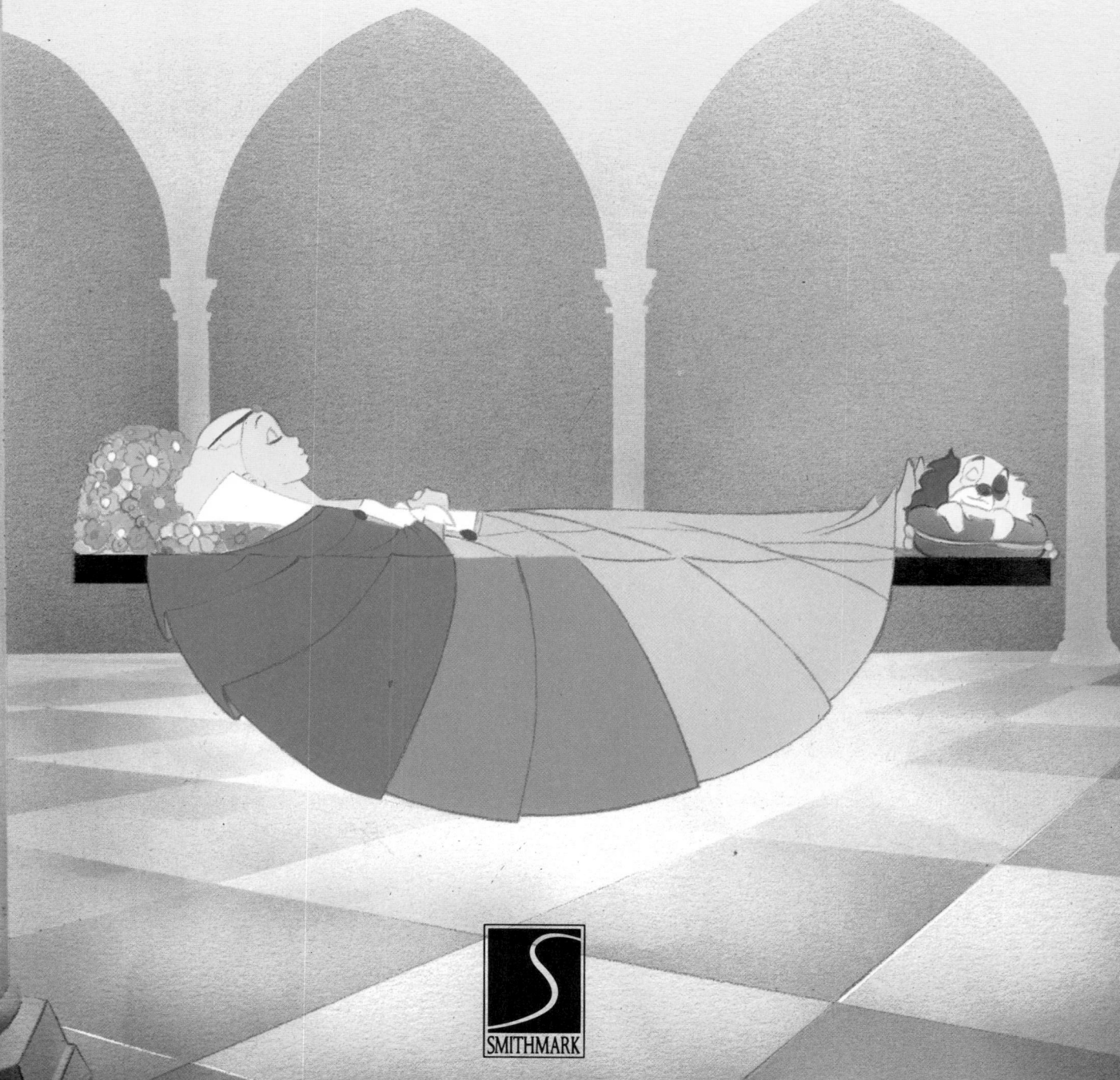

SMITHMARK

A very many years ago there lived a king and queen. Together they ruled wisely over their kingdom. Although they loved each other, they couldn't feel completely happy because they wanted very much to have a child. Their pet dog, Jester, brought them some happiness, but at night, when the dog and all the servants were asleep, the king and queen would sigh and wish for a child to brighten their castle.

One day the king and queen's dearest wish came true, and the queen gave birth to a lovely baby girl. The king danced merrily about the room, then rushed to his daughter's side. "You are so beautiful and precious!" he exclaimed to the sleeping baby. "We must have a royal party to invite all the fairies of the kingdom to meet you and share our happiness!"

The day was set for the party, the invitations went out, the royal cooks prepared a feast, and all was ready. On the day of the party the fairies flew into the castle, by various means, to celebrate the birth of the baby.

After the fairies peered into the cradle to see the sleeping baby, they took their seats at the banquet table. The king lifted his glass. "To a long and happy life for our little princess!" he proclaimed. The guests cheered and clapped.

Everyone at the party enjoyed the delicious feast, then danced to the music of a lively band. The king even danced with his baby in his arms. Then he gave each of the fairies a box of glittering jewels to thank them for coming.

15

But the joyful celebration was interrupted when the ballroom doors flew open and a scowling figure stormed across the floor. It was the evil and most powerful fairy of the kingdom. The king and queen had quite forgotten to invite her to the party. She glared angrily at the innocent baby, then turned to the other fairies. "Go ahead and give the child your gifts," she said. "And then I shall give mine!"

The king and queen and the fairies tried to carry on with the party, although the wicked fairy had spoiled the happy mood. One by one the fairies approached the baby princess, and bestowed their happy wishes. The smallest fairy hid behind the cradle.

Then the evil fairy stalked across the room. She scooped up the baby in her enormous hand, and as she bestowed her evil spell, the baby appeared as the beautiful woman she would become. "When you have grown to a young woman," uttered the fairy, "you will prick your thumb on a spindle, and will die!"

After the evil fairy stalked out of the castle, the smallest fairy stepped forward. "The evil fairy is so powerful that I cannot erase the spell, but I can soften it," she said. "Princess, when the spindle pricks your thumb you will not die, but shall sleep for a hundred years. After that only a prince's kiss may awaken you."

The king and queen were determined to protect their child from harm. The king sent his heralds throughout the kingdom, where they issued his royal proclamation that all spinning wheels be brought to the castle courtyard and burned.

The years passed and the baby grew into a lovely young woman. Her heart was kind and good, and she was loved by all. The king and queen had never told her of the evil fairy's spell. One day they set out to tour the kingdom, leaving the princess and Jester with the castle servants.

The princess, who loved to explore the castle, was delighted to discover a stairway she had never seen before.

Dreamily, she made her way up the stairs. The sunlight dissolved into a gloomy darkness at the top of the stairs, where a wooden door was shut tight. The curious princess could hear something on the other side of the door, and as she peeked through the keyhole and leaned against the door, it swung open.

In the cold, dark room on the other side of the door, an old woman, hidden in a cloak, sat spinning by candlelight. The princess watched, transfixed, for she had never seen a spinning wheel. Jester whimpered.

"Come closer," invited the woman. "Would you like to try it?"

The princess slowly crossed the room.

"Here, take this spindle," crooned the woman. But as the princess reached for the spindle, the sharp point pricked her thumb. At once sleepiness overcame the princess, who fell to her knees. The woman pushed back her hood, revealing the frightening face of the evil fairy.

Later that day, when the king and queen returned from their trip, their beloved daughter did not run out to greet them. Jester led them to the tower room, where they found their daughter on the floor by the spinning wheel. Sadly they lay the princess on her bed.

Then the queen ordered the royal messenger, with his seven-league boots, to summon the smallest fairy to the castle. The messenger bounded across the kingdom until he found the fairy. Then, wiping a tear from his face, he said, "You must come quickly! The princess has fallen under an evil spell."

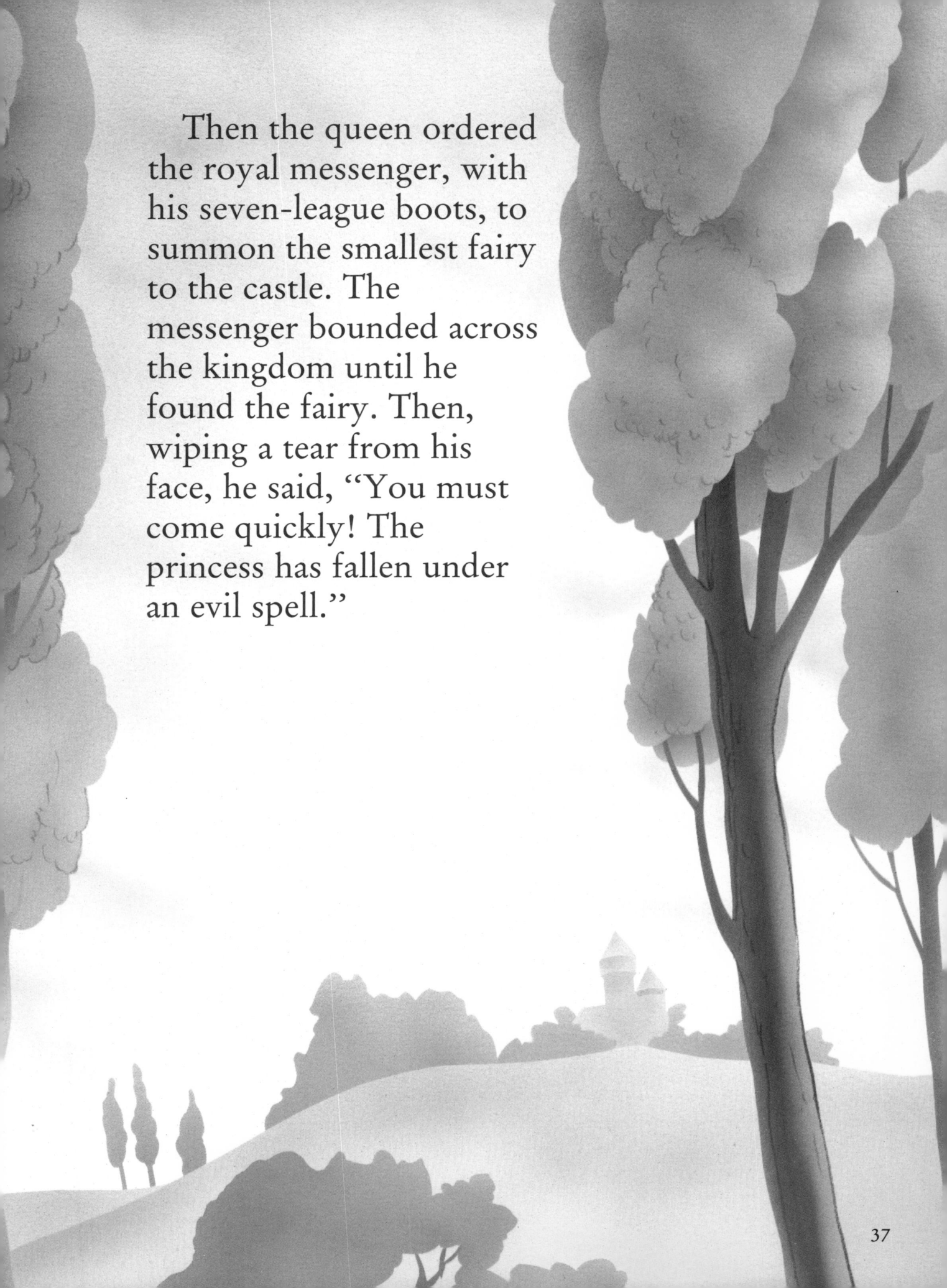

With her pet birds pulling the hem of her long dress, and the messenger balanced in her skirt, she flew to the castle. There she found the princess, grown to a woman and deep in a dreamless sleep, watched over by her unhappy parents.

The fairy flitted throughout the castle, casting a magic spell that put everyone into a deep slumber. The cooks with their pots and pans, the maids with their sewing and cleaning, the grooms with their horses, the butler in his pantry . . .

. . . the guards at the entrance, the ladies
in waiting – everyone was soon fast asleep.
"Now no one will age during the
princess's long sleep," said the fairy.

Night came, then day, and nothing
changed. A week passed, then a month,
then years came and went, and still all
slumbered on under the enchantment.
The trees grew, and vines climbed the
castle walls. A hundred years passed.

44

One day a prince from the nearby kingdom got lost in the mountains. He spied a castle in the distant woods, then came upon a peasant in his field, who told him the story of the sleeping princess. "But no one can enter that castle," he finished. "It is all grown over with brambles."

The prince decided to see for himself. "Surely it can't be true," he said to his horse. "I heard that story long ago. It's only a fairy tale!"

As the prince approached the castle, the thorny brambles flattened themselves to the ground by some strange magic. The prince walked over them with ease.

As soon as the prince pushed open the castle door, and stepped inside, he knew that the story was true. In every room people were frozen deep in sleep, wearing old-fashioned clothes and covered with dust and cobwebs.

The prince wandered through the castle until he came to the room of the slumbering princess. Sadly, he knelt by her bed. "You are a sleeping beauty," he whispered, overcome by her loveliness. Then he gave her a gentle kiss.

The princess sighed, then opened her eyes. "Who are you?" she asked. The prince told her who he was, and how he had come to be there, and the story of the fairy's wicked spell. While he spoke, the princess listened in wonder, and felt love growing in her heart.

When the prince had broken the spell with his kiss, everyone in the castle had also come to life. The king and queen rushed to their daughter's bed, where they were overjoyed to find the princess awake, and delighted to meet the prince who had ended the enchantment.

And it was decreed that on the seventh day the prince and princess would be married. Invitations were sent out to friends and family, and to the fairies of the kingdom. The king and queen noted, with satisfaction, the tenderness and love shared by the young couple.

All the kingdom rejoiced when the princess and prince were married. After the ceremony, lively music and dancing filled the castle with the merriest sounds in a hundred years. And the princess and prince lived together, in love and happiness, ever after.